SO-AIM-297

FRANKLIN PIERCE
COLLEGE LIBRARY
RINDGE, N.H. 03461

Legend of the Milky Way

RETOLD AND ILLUSTRATED BY JEANNE M. LEE

Henry Holt and Company · New York

Copyright © 1982 by Jeanne M. Lee
All rights reserved, including the right to reproduce this book or portions thereof in any form.
Published by Henry Holt and Company, Inc., 115 West 18th Street, New York, New York 10011.
Published in Canada by Fitzhenry & Whiteside Limited, 195 Allstate Parkway, Ontario L3R 4T8.

Library of Congress Cataloging in Publication Data
Lee, Jeanne M.   Legend of the Milky Way.
   Summary: Retells the Chinese legend of the Weaver Princess who came down from heaven to
marry a mortal, a love story represented in the stars of the Milky Way.
   [1. Folklore—China.   2. Stars—Fiction.   3. Milky Way—Fiction]   I. Title.
PZ8.1.L367Le   398.2'1'0951   [E]   81-6906

Henry Holt books are available at special discounts for bulk purchases for sales promotions,
premiums, fund-raising, or educational use. Special editions or book excerpts can also be created
to specification. For details contact: Special Sales Director,
Henry Holt & Co., Inc., 115 West 18th Street, New York, New York 10011

ISBN 0-8050-0217-0 (hardcover)   10   9   8   7   6   5
ISBN 0-8050-1361-X (paperback)   10   9   8   7   6   5   4   3
First published in hardcover in 1982 by Henry Holt and Company, Inc.
First Owlet edition 1990.

Printed in the United States of America

To Eric and Brian

The Chinese tell an ancient story about the Milky Way, which they call the "Silver River."

Long ago in a small village in China, a peasant boy lived
in a small house by the mountainside. His only friend
was his water buffalo; together they tilled the fields
from daybreak to sundown.

After work, the two friends relaxed on the riverbank.
While the buffalo swam, the boy played his flute.

The boy became a young man.

One evening as he sat playing his flute,
his music traveled up, up, up
to the heavenly courts.

The beautiful seventh daughter of the King of the Heavens, the weaver princess, heard it. The melody was sweet beyond words. Leaving her loom and the heavenly courts, she went down on the clouds in search of the sound.

"Who are you?" the young man asked.
"A weaver from far away,"
the princess answered.

They talked and sang through the night, and soon
the weaver princess forgot her heavenly home.

She married the earthly young man
and was happy with him in his small house.

One day, the old buffalo became sick.
"Dear master," the buffalo said before he died,
"when I am gone, sew my hide into a cloak.
It will perform miracles for you."

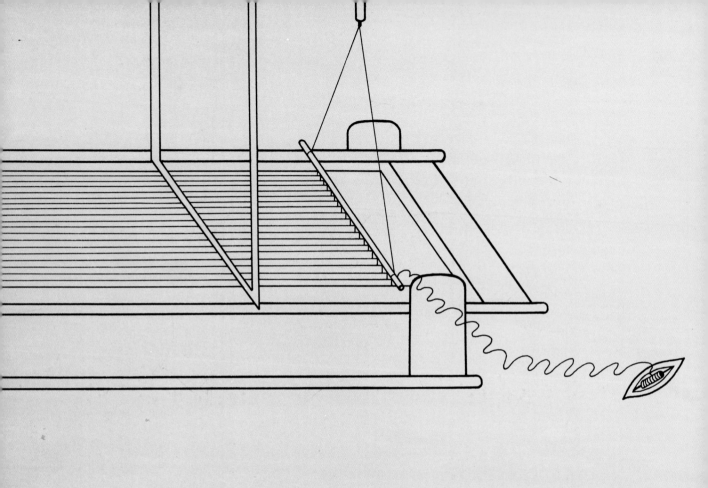

In the heavens, the Queen Mother
noticed the empty loom.
Angry, she ordered the heavenly
guards to search for the weaver princess.

They found her in her earthly home
and brought her back.

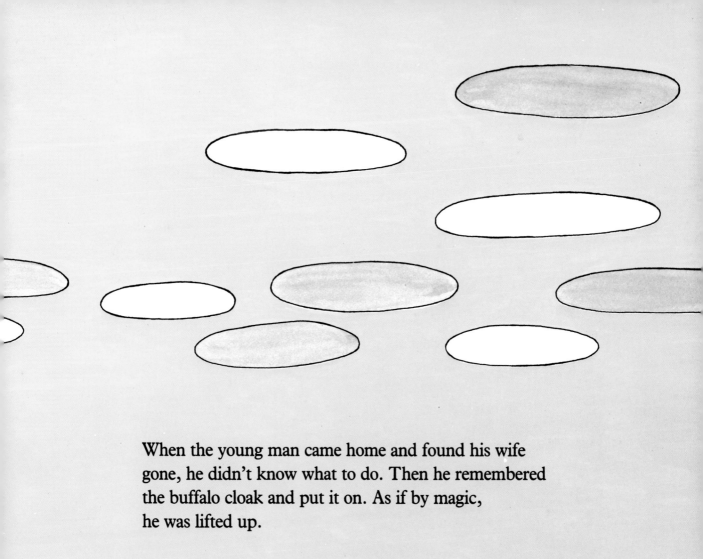

When the young man came home and found his wife
gone, he didn't know what to do. Then he remembered
the buffalo cloak and put it on. As if by magic,
he was lifted up.

The Queen Mother, who had been watching,
took a silver pin from her hair and drew
a silver river across the heavens to stop him.
He could go no further.

To separate the pair forever, the Queen Mother
turned them into stars, one on each side of the river.

The unhappy princess cried
from morning until night.

Her father, the King of the Heavens, took pity on her.
He persuaded the Queen to allow the couple
to visit each other once a year.

And each year, on the seventh day of the seventh month, the
blackbirds of the heavens form themselves into a bridge across
the Silver River, and the weaver princess crosses over
to visit her earthly husband. They talk and sing for a while,
then she rushes back lest the Queen Mother punish her.

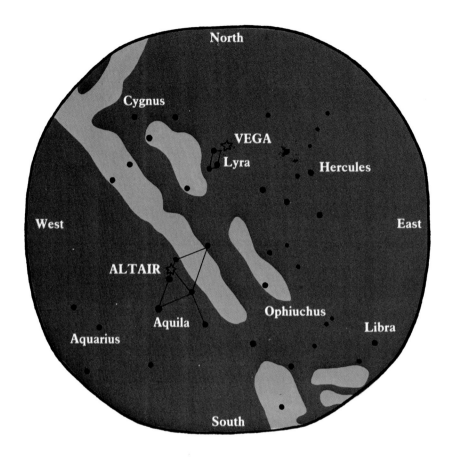

The seventh day of the seventh month of the Chinese year falls sometime in August. On that day in China, the people honor the weaver princess and her earthly husband with a feast. If it rains that night, they say the princess is crying because she must say good-bye to her husband.

Sometimes, on a clear night, you can see the bridge of birds across the "Silver River." The star that astronomers call *Vega* in the constellation *Lyra* is the weaver princess, and the star *Altair* in the constellation *Aquila* is the young man.